Good night,
reindeer.

Good Night, Reindeer

Written by Denise Brennan-Nelson
Illustrated by Marco Bucci

Time for bed.
Good night, Vixen.

Good night, Prancer.
Good night, hooves.

**Good night, Dancer.
Good night, shoes.**

Good night, Comet.
Good night, stars.
Good night, planets.
Good night, cars.
Good night, cookies.
Good night, toys.

Good night, Cupid.
Good night, noise.

Good night, Donner.
Good night, day.

Good night, Dasher.

Good night, sleigh.

Good night, workshop.
Good night, elves.

Good night, dolls.

Good night, bells.

Good night, Rudolph.
Good night, good night.

Time for bed.
Turn off your light…

GOOD NIGHT,
Rudolph!

For Emma and Owen.

—Denise

★

For my Mom, who loved to read Christmas books to me when I was little.

—Marco

Text Copyright © 2017 Denise Brennan-Nelson
Illustration Copyright © 2017 Marco Bucci
Design Copyright © 2017 Sleeping Bear Press

Sleeping Bear Press
2395 South Huron Parkway, Suite 200
Ann Arbor, MI 48104
www.sleepingbearpress.com

Printed and bound in the United States.

10 9 8 7 6 5

Library of Congress Cataloging-in-Publication Data

Names: Brennan-Nelson, Denise, author. | Bucci, Marco, illustrator.
Title: Good night, reindeer / written by Denise Brennan-Nelson ; illlustrated
by Marco Bucci.
Description: Ann Arbor, MI : Sleeping Bear Press, [2017] | Summary:
Santa checks in on all his reindeer to make sure they are tucked
in for the night before their big Christmas day.
Identifiers: LCCN 2017006727 | ISBN 9781585363704
Subjects: | CYAC: Stories in rhyme. | Reindeer—Fiction. | Bedtime—Fiction.
| Christmas—Fiction.
Classification: LCC PZ8.3.B7457 Go 2017 | DDC [E]—dc23
LC record available at https://lccn.loc.gov/2017006727